D0191723

WITHDRAWN

for my Grandparents, E.P.

FAR
FAR
AWAY
BOOKS

Sylvester
and the New Year

inspired by a tale told by Eduard Mörike

illustrated by Emmeline Pidgen

On the last evening of December, millions of twinkling stars filled the sky as Clara and her father walked joyfully through the snow.

Crunch, crunch, crunch, went their boots.

"Look, Father!" pointed Clara.
"The moonlight makes the snow sparkle.
It paints everything silver."

"That reminds me of a story I know, about silver moon horses and starry skies," he replied.

"Tell me, please!" urged Clara.

"All right," her father laughed,

"and by the time
I have finished,
we shall be home."

And so, between the
snow and the **stars**,
Clara's father began...

"**Far, far away,**

much further than you can
see, there is a little cottage.

To get there you have to travel

up, and up, and up ...

past all the stars in the Milky Way...

... until a pair of

silver gates

appear, leading to a

magical garden.

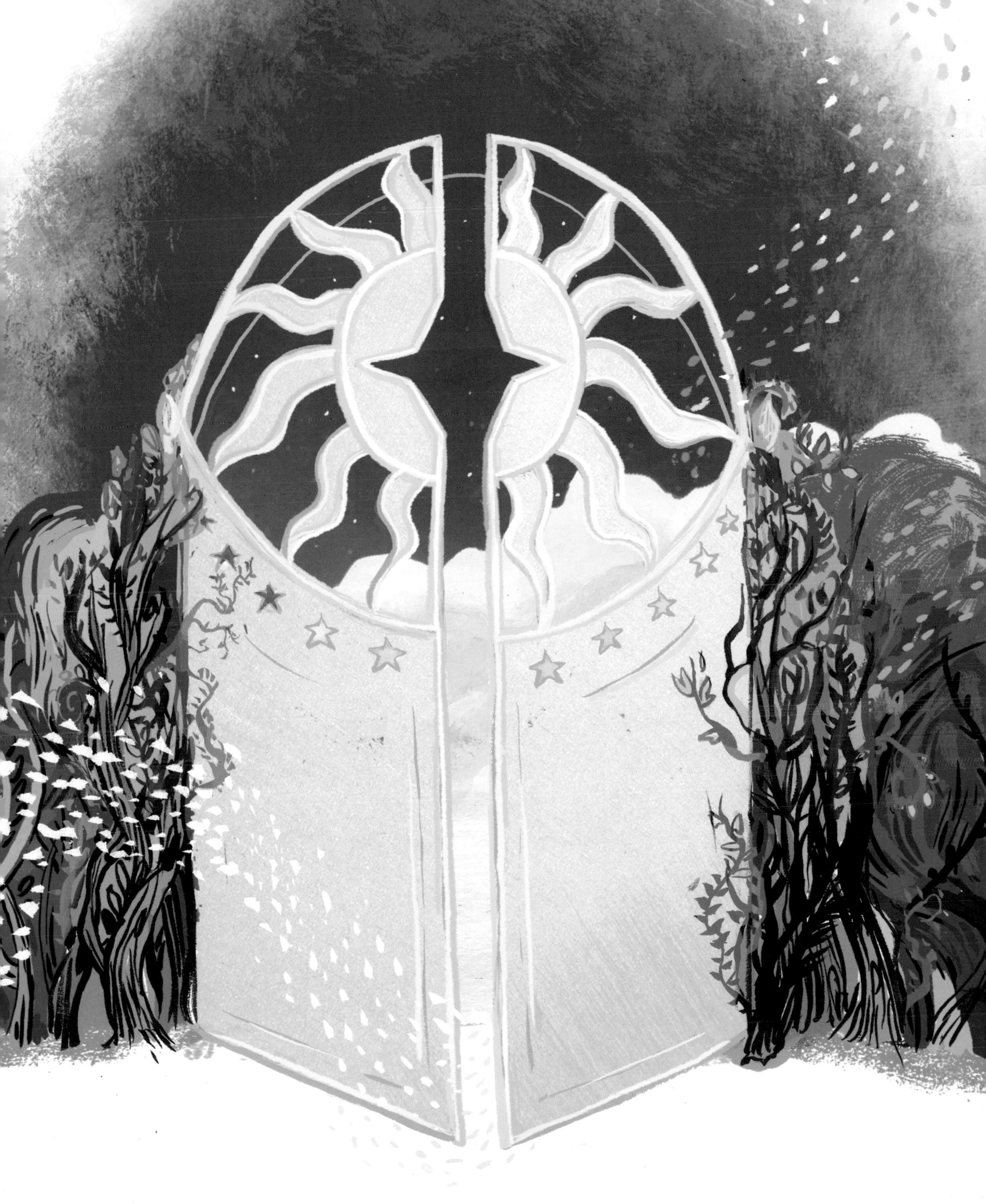

Just before these gates are
rolling cloud meadows,
where angels stand watch over
glittering sky lambs.

Within sight, four white horses
prance and **play** in a fine paddock.

They are **silver moon horses**
and when they jump, sparks of moonlight
fly from their hooves.

Past the paddock, there is a small gate, and at last, a path that leads to the little cottage, where a deep rumbling noise floats through its open window.

'SnOOOOore'

Inside, Sylvester is fast asleep.

His bed of **glittering starlight** is so comfortable
that he sleeps all year long until New Year's Eve, when an
angel comes to wake him.

Knock, knock, knock.

'Wake up, Sylvester. Wake up! It is time!'

Under the bedcovers, Sylvester grumbles.

'Eh? What? Already?'

Groggy with sleep he awakens to
find a gleaming angel boy at his door.

'Hurry Sylvester, it's time,'

repeats the angel.

'Yes, yes,' chuckles Sylvester,
'I am on my way.'

Sylvester hurries to dress.

He wraps himself in a thick, fleecy coat and pulls on warm, padded boots. Then he tucks a **beautiful silver hammer** under his **wide silver belt.**

Stepping out
into the paddock,
the **moon horses**
gallop over to greet him.

Sylvester hitches them
to a magnificent
gold and silver sleigh.

The horses paw the ground, sending sparkling moonlight from their hooves. They shake their heads impatiently in a shower of moondust spray.

'Fly on!' cries Sylvester. The horses gallop as fast as the wind, through the rolling cloud meadows to the silver gates of the magical garden.

When they arrive, Sylvester climbs from his sleigh
and lifts his silver hammer to knock three times.

Knock, knock, knock!

The thump of the hammer rings like a great
bell and the gates swing open. A dazzling angel
appears, glittering like sunlight upon water.

He is the gatekeeper.

'Greetings, Sylvester.
Come, let us fetch
the New Year.'

The gatekeeper leads Sylvester
to the edge of a sparkling stream.

It is the River of Life.

'Child,' calls the angel, 'it is time.'

He reaches out to a cheerful boy and helps
him out of the water.

'Take the New Year Child to Earth, Sylvester, and bring the Old Year back to me,' says the angel.

Sylvester gently lifts the little boy into the sleigh.

'Fly on!' calls Sylvester. He flicks his reins and his moon horses race across the Milky Way, their silver manes scattering moonshine and their hooves flashing between the stars.

And so they gallop, down to the gates of Earth.

Down, and down, and down.

When they arrive, Sylvester takes out his silver hammer and knocks twelve times on the gates of Earth. On the twelfth knock, the gates burst open to the joyous chimes of bells, ringing all across the World.

Ding, dong, ding, dong, ding, ding, dong!

The New Year Child jumps from the sleigh and runs eagerly through the open gates. Fireworks and laughter float through the air as Earth welcomes the New Year.

An old man sits in the shadow of the gates.
When he sees Sylvester, he sighs.

'Sylvester, don't you recognise me?'

he asks.

'Of course, dear friend,
You are the Old Year,'

replies Sylvester.

The Old Year stands up wearily.
So many things have happened
during his year on Earth that
he now appears very old.

'Never mind. You'll be young again in the twinkling of a star,' smiles Sylvester, as he gently leads the Old Year to the sleigh.

In a trice, the horses speed them far, far away, back through the Milky Way to the gates of the magical garden, where the angel gatekeeper greets them.

'Welcome home,
Old Year,'

the angel smiles.

He carries the old man
in his strong arms down
to the sparkling stream.

The Old Year lowers his frail body
into the glittering water as the
River of Life washes time away.

'Soon you will return to Earth
again as the New Year!' calls Sylvester.

The Old Year smiles and waves goodbye.

Sylvester climbs back into his sleigh.

'Fly on,' he calls once more, and his moon horses gallop gladly home.

When they reach their paddock, he scatters star grass in their stalls and covers them with cloud blankets to keep them warm.

His work well done, Sylvester returns to his cottage to eat his favourite meal and goes back to bed, to sleep for another year."

Clara's father ended the story just as they reached their home.

"Father, does Sylvester really bring a New Year to Earth every year?"

Clara asked.

"Oh yes, every year," her father nodded.

"If you listen carefully, you will hear the bells
and fireworks, as the New Year Child arrives."

Clara snuggled down into her cosy bed. As she
closed her eyes, she was sure she heard Sylvester's
hammer knocking on the gates.

"Welcome, New Year Child,"

she whispered, as she drifted off between
the stars, dreaming of the year ahead.

...Wishing you a
Happy New Year,
filled with magic
and dreams come true!

Our story "Sylvester and the New Year" is inspired by a fairytale told to a little girl more than a 100 years ago.

Originally told in German, and passed down through generations, Far Far Away Books now proudly presents a modern incarnation of this classic story. Together with the magical illustrations of Emmeline Pidgen, it will charm readers of all ages for generations to come.

We hope that "Sylvester and the New Year" will become part of your family's New Year tradition, and that it will delight your children as it once delighted a little girl in Germany so many years ago.

First published in Great Britain in 2012
by Far Far Away Books and Media Ltd.
20-22 Bedford Row, London WC1R 4JS

Copyright 2012 Far Far Away Books and Production Lda.

Inspired by the fairytale originally told by Eduard Mörike,
who died in 1875.

The moral rights of Emmeline Pidgen to be identified
as the illustrator of this work have been asserted.

ISBN: 978-1-908786-06-7 (hardback)
ISBN: 978-1-908786-66-1 (paperback)

A CIP catalogue record for this book
is available from the British Library.

Designed at www.aitchcreative.co.uk

Printed and bound in Portugal
by Printer Portuguesa

All Far Far Away Books can be ordered from
www.centralbooks.com

www.farfarawaybooks.com